PUFFIN BOOKS

FINN MAC COOL

AND THE SMALL MEN OF DEEDS

The King and Queen of the giants are in great distress. Every time a baby Prince is born, he disappears again that same night, snatched mysteriously away from them despite the highest vigilance. The giants' only hope lies in Finn Mac Cool, the bravest, wisest, tallest and rudest of the warriors of the Fianna, who just happens that day to be afflicted with a terrible headache.

When poor Finn encounters the seven small men of deeds he is at first sceptical, but his headache is magically taken away from him by Taking Easy and he realizes that his only chance of success in this latest challenge lies with these strange new friends.

Narrated with warmth and humour, this eccentric tale with its traditional Celtic illustrations will delight young and old alike.

Pat O'Shea was born in Galway, Ireland, and came to England for a holiday when she was eighteen. Since then it has always been her home. She spent thirteen years writing her first children's novel, *The Hounds of the Mórrigan*. She now lives in Manchester and visits Ireland whenever she can.

Also by Pat O'Shea

THE HOUNDS OF THE MÓRRÍGAN

FINN
MAC COOL
AND THE SMALL MEN OF DEEDS

RETOLD BY

Pat O'Shea

ILLUSTRATED BY
STEPHEN LAVIS

PUFFIN BOOKS

PUFFIN BOOKS

Published by the Penguin Group
27 Wrights Lane, London w8 5tz, England
Viking Penguin Inc., 40 West 23rd Street, New York, New York 10010, USA
Penguin Books Australia Ltd, Ringwood, Victoria, Australia
Penguin Books Canada Ltd, 2801 John Street, Markham, Ontario, Canada l3r 1b4
Penguin Books (NZ) Ltd, 182–190 Wairau Road, Auckland 10, New Zealand

Penguin Books Ltd, Registered Offices: Harmondsworth, Middlesex, England

First published by Oxford University Press 1987
Published in Puffin Books 1990
1 3 5 7 9 10 8 6 4 2

Made and printed in Great Britain by
Richard Clay Ltd, Bungay, Suffolk
Filmset in Monophoto Baskerville

AUTHOR'S NOTE

For ease of reading I have changed the Gaelic spelling of the hero's name Fionn MacCumaill, to Finn Mac Cool – which is how it is pronounced.

*In memory of
my mother and father
and my brother Joe*

WHEN Cormac Mac Art was High King of Ireland many, many hundreds of years ago, he had a standing army of fighting men, known as the Fianna. They were all warriors of great renown, they were poets, they were kind-hearted to the young, the old and the weak; and they sat as much as they stood, for there wasn't a lot of warring going on during their time. As they were big and strong and hardy in all weathers, they preferred the camp and life in the open air to the fort or the house; and they lived outdoors all the year through. Loving to travel as well, they spent a few months in one place and a few months in another place as the whim took hold of them and, with things being so quiet, it didn't matter to the High King; and anyway, runners could always be sent to get the Fianna, if they were needed. Their daily lives were to be envied, for they spent their time mostly in hunting and making rhymes, and bragging and having picnics.

There were times when the Norsemen came in their long boats and the Fianna would always be there to meet them, laughing and beckoning and blowing kisses, and calling them to come ashore and have a picnic. All the while, the sharp points of their spears would be flashing in the sun and their swords would be dancing brightly in their hands and they'd be doing staggering tricks with their slingshots, to amuse the strangers.

But the Norsemen would answer that they were fully qualified pillagers and arsonists, and that they hadn't gone to all the trouble of building boats and working themselves up for mayhem and murder and come all that distance just to go on old picnics; and they would explain that they hadn't sailed and rowed across oceans for hard-boiled eggs. The Norsemen used to work themselves up for mayhem and murder when sitting round their great winter fires, toasting at the front while their backs were freezing, listening to stories of how their fathers and grandfathers were this, that, and the other for courage and valour and stuff like that, and they used to go green with jealousy and be filled with the desire to carry on the family business. They would distinguish themselves by extinguishing others and become celebrities themselves, they all said dutifully.

So they used to be very annoyed when the Fianna shouted to them from the shore. They would answer then, that they hadn't the slightest intention of going where they were invited for they had better manners, that the Fianna must be intoxicated, that they had insulted the Norsemen's dignity, and that they, the proud Norsemen, would now go somewhere else to commit felonies and do grievous bodily harm and that, anyway, picnics weren't sophisticated.

They used to be angry as well because they always loved sneaking into estuaries and harbours, secretly and silently, to give everyone a surprise, and the Fianna always stopped them having this boyish and innocent bit of fun and would spoil everything. They would sail away then, swearing many strong and strange oaths, and they would go off to some other place to get presents for their wives, do a bit of slewing and be berserk in peace.

And the Fianna would shout after them:

'We like your funny hats with the cows' horns!' And they would make terrible jokes like:

'Come back an udder time!'

And they would moo like cows and shout for two pints, please; until the Norsemen's boats were out of sight.

And that is what life for the Fianna was like.

The Chief of them all was Finn Mac Cool and he was the tallest, the bravest and the wisest and, when necessary, the one who was most rude to the Men of the North. He was part Otherworld from his mother's side of the family; but, like anything with a bit of humanity in it, he wasn't perfect. His greatest fault, some might say, was that he couldn't bear being unwell, at all.

In the early morning of one lovely day, Gariv Cronan, the old servant of Finn Mac Cool, went to his master's tent and lifted the flap.

'Hail, Finn,' he said brightly.

'Mornin',' Finn whispered without turning his head and with the barest movement of his lips.

'Rise up, O Mighty Chieftain,' said Gariv. 'The day is here, the cooking fires

are lit and all tents are open to the light but yours.'

But Finn was sullen.

'Go away,' he muttered through clenched teeth.

'Drink a sup of this lovely milk, my darling; and then get out of bed and come to your breakfast,' Gariv said winningly and he came inside the tent.

'If you come any nearer, I'll bite you,' Finn said in a hiss and without opening his eyes.

'You are slothful,' said Gariv, changing his tack. 'Get up!'

'I am not slothful and I won't get up,' Finn answered peevishly, still lying as stiff as a board.

'Don't be so contrary!'

'I'm not contrary.'

'You are, you always were and you always will be contrary,' Gariv said, and warming to his theme, he added: 'You were a contrary child!'

'I was not.'

'You were a child that would never get dressed but came down in your shift every morning. And you'd be told: "Go and put on your traps this minute, you bold little brat, or you'll catch your death of pneumonia!"; and you'd come down the next moment wearing one shoe and the shift gone and your chubby legs blue with the cold. That's what you were like!'

'Wasn't!' mumbled Finn.

'Come out of it and don't be lying there mumbling to yourself like an old woman that has lost her teeth with her youth,' Gariv said crossly.

'You've an awful big mouth,' Finn observed and he didn't stir a muscle.

'You're an unnatural savage,' Gariv insulted him back.

'Don't slam that tent flap as you go out,' Finn warned him.

'You're a disputatious sourface, that's what you are,' Gariv complained and he left the tent, being careful to let the flap drop inch by quiet inch, for he loved Finn.

'You did that on purpose!' Finn moaned and he clutched his head and now that he was alone, he groaned from his soul. He lifted an eyelid to look at the world and, in the eye that looked out, pain swam like a fish.

By this time, the men of the Fianna were gathered outside.

'What's wrong with the Chief?' asked Caelte Mac Ronan.

'He's like a bag of cats and the father of all cats this morning and that's all I can say,' Gariv answered and he snapped his mouth shut tight.

Then Oisín, who was Finn's one and only son and his beloved, called into the tent.

'Finn! The day moves on and we are for two hours at feats of arms and then we are for the hunt. We are waiting for you.'

Finn moaned softly but made no other reply.

Then Oscar, who was Finn's one and only grandson and the apple of his eye, called into the tent.

'If you love us, get up, Finn,' he said.

But Finn answered:

'I'll love you tomorrow. Leave me alone today.'

'What's wrong with you at all?' asked Red-Haired Dermot.

'I am in a stew of pain,' Finn groaned.

'What kind of pain?' Gariv asked tenderly, as he at once regretted his pert conversation with his sick master.

'Inside the shell of my head, there are wild things playing jigs with hammers on the skin of my brain,' said Finn and he waited for sympathy.

'Is that all?' said Gariv, his voice rising in shock.

'Is that all?' the others echoed with the same amazement.

'I thought that you were in love the way you were going on,' said Dermot.

'And I feared that it was old age that had its miserable hold on him,' Caelte whispered, looking from one to the other of his companions with wonder.

'You've only a headache. What a baby you are,' said Gariv.

No answer from Finn.

'If word of this ever crosses the sea and reaches the ears of the Norsemen, there'll be queer talk about you,' Gariv admonished him.

Now Finn growled.

'No feats of arms this morning,' he suggested with menacing gentleness. 'Go away and hunt by yourselves for I'm no use at all today. And no more talk from Gariv!'

'It must be a bad headache,' Oisín said then.

The men fell to whispering among themselves about what to do with the day. It was greatly disappointing to them that Finn would not be with them whatever they decided upon. In the end they agreed that there would be no feats of arms, for the clash of weapons would be too great for their Chieftain to bear, but that they would wait for two hours

16

before going to hunt, in case the headache lifted and Finn got better. Then he can come with us, they said to each other and they smiled.

Within his tent, Finn wished from his heart that they would just go away. He wished that he could give them all a good tongue-lashing for the racket they were making with their sibilant hissing of gab, but the tongue lives in the head and that house was possessed by pain and Finn dared not speak more than was necessary and even that was too much.

Now for the Fianna, there was time to kill. This was something that they were not skilled at, though they knew that all that was needed was patience. Each man tried in his own way.

Of those that sat on hummocks, one scratched his knee, another counted all the toes that peeped through the short spears of green grass, two twisted strands of their hair into curls round slowly turning forefingers and some yawned. One sat with his chin resting on his hunched up knees and blinked from time to time and that was all. Yet another sat with his knees up but thrown apart to make a lap of his tunic skirt, where he dropped daisy petals one by one. Two played Piggy Going To Market; and a few played Cat's Cradle – and one tried to balance a blade of grass on the tip of his nose. A few of the Fianna stood around

leaning on the shafts of their spears, while they looked into the distance at nothing, and a lone but notable warrior stood like that but with one leg tucked behind the knee of the other while he tried to think out a poem, but he lacked the mood. All sighed. All were bored.

'If only a few of those funny Norsemen would come, even – we'd have a few laughs at least,' muttered Caelte.

At this one warrior got to his feet and made a good sprint to the shore, but when he came back after a while, he said listlessly:

'There isn't one! Not a sight of one!'

And Dermot said with a profound sigh:

'You can never find one when you want one!'

And all were agreed on that.

Some time later, Oscar spoke:

'Well, he won't be coming today,' he said.

Everyone knew that he was talking about Finn.

'We'll have to go without him,' said Conan.

'I don't know,' sighed a third. 'I haven't the heart for it, somehow.'

'And how will you feel tonight when your mouth is full of hunger and nothing else?' Caelte asked him.

'You are right, Caelte,' everyone said, much relieved. 'We'd better make a start, so.'

They called their hounds to them and the sitting ones rose to their feet and they all set off at a trot, brightening up with every yard they covered, for they loved to run bare-footed on the earth.

In a little while they were gone, and that is how it came to pass that Finn Mac Cool was alone but for Gariv when the giant came to call.

◆

It was in the quiet of the early afternoon that Gariv, coming back with two wooden buckets of spring water slopping on his legs, saw the giant. The big man was sitting on one of the hummocks gazing sorrowfully at the seemingly deserted camp of the Fianna. The flaps of all the tents were opened wide and pinned back to let in the fresh air, the cooking fires were low, and there wasn't a soul to be seen anywhere. In the first shock of seeing him, Gariv almost dropped the buckets, but he bethought himself of Finn's headache just in time and he stood wondering and looking at

the giant.

The giant struck himself on the breast, and he discharged a powerful, moaning sigh.

'Too late, too late. All is lost. Oh, my poor King,' he said.

Gariv wondered even more at this, but he stood very still and held his peace a little longer.

He saw the giant take the hem of his tunic to his eyes and perform dabbing motions with it and when the giant spoke again, his voice was choked with tears.

'Without Finn's help, what are we to do?' he spluttered and he covered his face with his skirt.

Emboldened by these signs of sorrow, Gariv went up to the giant and said:

'What do you want here, my good man?'

He waited in trepidation for the giant's response.

The giant uncovered his face and looked at Gariv very mournfully. Gariv instantly regained his nerve.

'Well, my good man?' he said. 'Have you no tongue in your head?'

'I come in search of Finn Mac Cool,' the giant began and was cut short by Gariv.

'Finn Mac Cool, Mac Baiscne,' he said, giving the giant a short lesson in genealogy.

'Your pardon,' said the giant.

'Granted. Tell me why you seek the great Finn.'

'Are you Finn?' the giant asked hopefully.

Gariv was flattered. For a moment he seemed to swell.

'I might be,' he answered cautiously. 'Tell me, anyway.'

'My full story I'll tell only to Finn. But to anyone else I'll say this – my King is in a desperate state and is in sore need of help and humanity from someone – and who better than Finn?'

'Who indeed?' Gariv agreed proudly.

'But I'm too late,' continued the giant. 'They've all gone off gallivanting for the day; and if Finn is to help, he must help before nightfall and he'll hardly be back from the hunt before then.'

'Come with me,' Gariv said peremptorily. 'Walk softly!'

The giant got up and followed Gariv.

They hadn't gone but a step or two, when Gariv said:

'You can carry the buckets!'

This the giant did so readily and gently that Gariv was almost ashamed of himself.

When they reached Finn's tent, Gariv stuck his head inside.

'There's a giant out here, come to visit you, Finn,' he called, as though he were telling the most natural thing in the world.

'Gariv! You'd sink to any low trick to get me up. No more! Or I'll send you from me without a reference,' Finn tried to growl, but it came out all self-sorrowful and not at all strong.

'No trick,' said the giant in his deep voice. And bad as he was with pain, Finn started up to grab a weapon to defend Gariv, himself and the camp.

'Hail to you, Finn; please don't disturb yourself,' the giant said politely.

'Hail,' Finn groaned back. 'Have you come to fight me or to try for tribute?'

'No, indeed, Finn. Far from it.'

'That's good,' Finn said weakly, and he lay back on his bed and sheathed his eyes with his eyelids.

'The King of my race has heard of the deeds of Finn Mac Cool,' began the giant.

'High deeds,' Gariv whispered encouragingly.

'The high deeds of Finn Mac Cool,' the giant said, nodding. 'And he has sent me here with a message.'

Finn was wincing at the strength of the big man's voice, but he was too well-mannered to rebuke a stranger for what he could not help.

'He was wondering,' the giant said diffidently, 'if you would help him out in his dire trouble, if you have any love in you.'

'I have my share; but not today,' Finn said. 'All I have today is pain and anger and the never-ending tedium of Gariv's companionship.'

Gariv folded his arms across his chest, stuck his nose up in the air and said:

'Rubbish!' very sharply and quickly.

'I'm sorry for your pain. Indeed I'm sorry for it, when my poor King is at his wit's end. He asks most humbly if you would come and guard his child that was born this morning.'

'Guard his child?' Gariv said in astonishment. He dropped his arms. 'Are they all as big as you in your country?' he asked.

'They are.'

'Couldn't you guard the child yourselves?'

'Ah, if only we could! A thief will come

23

tonight and steal him away. The same evil thief has already stolen two sons that were born to our King and his heart-broken Queen. Lovely little lads they were, and each one snatched on the night of the day of his birth. Only one day old and snatched!'

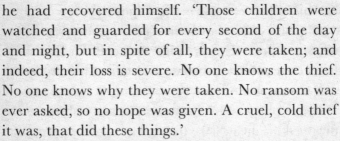

Here the giant burst into tears and held up the already sodden skirt of his tunic to receive them.

'There, there,' Gariv said most kindly, and he patted him.

'Those children,' said the giant when he had recovered himself. 'Those children were watched and guarded for every second of the day and night, but in spite of all, they were taken; and indeed, their loss is severe. No one knows the thief. No one knows why they were taken. No ransom was ever asked, so no hope was given. A cruel, cold thief it was, that did these things.'

One more sob escaped the giant.

There was silence then as Finn's words were awaited to fill an ever-lengthening gap.

Finn thought of his own son Oisín reared to

manhood and he thought of his grandson Oscar and how sweet he was. He remembered that he had said that he would love Oscar tomorrow but not today; and he knew that he was lucky to be able to say such a thing. Pity for the King filled his heart, but the pain in his head suddenly grew fiercer and he mumbled:

'My shame! I am not able for any deed today. I'll come tomorrow, good big man.'

'He gives twice who gives quickly,' Gariv murmured sarcastically, inventing an old saying on the spot.

'Tomorrow will be too late,' the giant said. 'For why can you not come today?'

'I am sick to my soul with a headache,' Finn said. He knew as he said it that it sounded like a weak excuse, and he was deeply embarrassed, and glad that his eyes were shut so that he could not see the giant's face which was, no doubt, showing contempt.

But the giant was only concerned about Finn's pain and anxious that it should be cured for everyone's sake.

'Did you try a hot nettle poultice stitched into a salmon skin?' he asked.

'He did not,' said Gariv. 'Nor would he, not if he was to be boiled for it!'

'Did you try hunting it out with a hot iron to the temple?'

'He wouldn't. Not for a saint,' said Gariv.

'Will he try anything at all?' the giant asked the servant, turning away from Finn.

'That man? If you asked him to put on his shirt – he'd take off his shoes!' Gariv said, committing calumny without caring a scratch.

'I'd best be going,' the giant said, rising on one knee. He had been kneeling in meekness outside the tent, with his head bowed low to hear Finn's words.

'Wait,' said Finn, who was deeply ashamed. 'I'll come as soon as I'm better. Or if the headache doesn't leave me at all – I'll follow after you in less than an hour.'

'Is that your word?'

'It is.'

'Thank you, Finn. A million thanks to you,' the giant said, and he went away.

After a few moments, Finn said, as he struggled to think through his headache:

'Run after that big man and ask him where his country is, Mighty Mouth!'

And Gariv hurried to go after the giant.

'It's seven leagues and a bit over the sea,' he said when he came back.

'You're a great help!' Finn said and he struggled off his bed. He put himself tenderly into his tunic and cloak, hardly moving his throbbing head.

'What are you doing?' Gariv asked slyly.

'I'm going after that big man. I'm going down to the shore to ask him the way to his country. I'm doing your work,' Finn growled, and he set off.

'The sea breeze might do you good,' Gariv called after him. 'Something must!'

Then he sat down and chuckled to himself. He admired himself for the clever way that he had got Finn up, after all. Sometimes you can do a great deal by keeping your mouth shut, he told himself cheerfully; for he had deliberately not asked the big man the way to his country, knowing full well that Finn would then have no option but to get up and follow after him. A good servant may sometimes be sly in his master's best interests, he said, and he lay down to have a rest. Finn's best treasure is his good name, he thought drowsily. He went to sleep, laughing.

◆

Finn had no trouble in following the way that the giant had gone, for the tracks of his feet were plain in the flattened grass. Even though the grass where Finn walked was of the thick, short, soft kind, he felt as if he were walking an iron road as every step seemed to jangle in his head. Even when he reached the wide shore and walked on the softest sand, things were no better, and he wasn't pleased to find that the strand was deserted and no sign of the giant but the hollows made by his feet in the sand, as if cows had nested in parallel broken lines all the way to the water's edge.

He stood and gazed out to the broad sweep of the horizon. There wasn't the merest glimpse of a boat or even the tip of a sail to be seen. Slowly and carefully and with his head held rigidly, he crouched and filled his cupped hands with water and splashed it on his face, but there was no refreshment in it for the sea was too warm. Cautiously he stood up again and once more his gaze travelled the ocean. The sunlight danced and flashed on the surface of the wide sea so Finn withdrew his still hurting gaze from it and turned to land. From the glare of the sun on the water and with the pain still in his head, everything swam before his eyes and he saw red mists and green mists and nothing else.

'Oh,' he groaned, and the mists cleared.

And there before him on the strand was a row of little men; and they were all smiling.

What in the world have we here, he wondered.

The small men bowed and one said:

'Hail to you, Finn Mac Cool, Mac Baiscne.'

'Good day to you,' Finn answered. He stared at them.

Nothing more was said for a while and then Finn bethought himself of his manners and what was due to others from one such as himself, and he asked:

'Who are you at all and how do you make your way in the world?'

'We are brothers. We each have a talent and all the talents are different,' the same small man answered.

'That's always handy in a big family,' Finn said politely. 'What is your talent and what is your name?'

'I can hear anything – there's nothing I can't hear. I can hear a spider turning over in its sleep in the corner of a house in far-away Lapland; I can hear a mouse cough in Arabia; I can hear the tongue of a sheep licking her new born lamb in a place called Thracia. The lamb is weak and I can hear its blood trying to be stronger.'

'And your name?' Finn asked, with the merest curving of his lips in a smile.

'My name is Hearing Ear.'

'I'm not at all surprised,' Finn said. 'Tell me what you do,' he said to the next small man.

'I can feel everything. I can feel with the stick as it shrivels in the fire; I can feel with the voice-box in a linnet's throat as she sings in the morning in a forest in Alba; I can feel with the little maggot whose body is like the thread of a screw as it burrows in a tree in the far eastern world.'

'Your name?' said Finn.

'Far Feeler!'

'There's sense in that,' Finn said, and he would have laughed but for the pain still throbbing in his head.

'What about you?' he asked the third small man.

'I am Knowing Man. I know what is going to happen in every part of the world.'

'Is that all?' asked Finn.

30

'It's enough!' Knowing Man replied.

'Your turn now,' Finn said to the fourth small man.

'I am a deadly shot with a bow. I can split a hair in two long even halves at a distance of twenty miles. I can loose a shower of arrows at the beginning of a second and have the sun's light blotted out by them, before that second reaches its end.'

'What name do they give you?'

'Bowman.'

'They understated you in your naming,' said Finn.

'Thank you,' Bowman replied.

'You are all telling me very great whoppers!' said Finn.

'We are not,' said Knowing Man.

'No more boasting now,' Finn said sternly.

'No boast at all,' said Far Feeler.

'It's a boast,' Finn insisted.

'It's not,' Bowman replied.

'Pride goes before a fall,' Finn warned.

'Indeed it does; but plain honesty has no such train-bearer,' Hearing Ear said.

'Do you say that you are honest?' Finn asked of the next small man.

'I am an honest thief. I am a very great thief,' the small man answered. 'I can steal the harper's harp without him knowing at all that it was gone, and he would still stroke the air with his fingers and fancy that he could still hear music, but it would only be in his head; I can steal a talon from the claw of a wide-awake eagle, and his brilliant eyes would not see me, nor would his sharp ear hear me, and he wouldn't know that it was missing until he tried to scratch his head. I could even steal the twinkle from your eye,' the small man finished and he smiled.

'Don't do that,' Finn said, alarmed.

'I wouldn't, for I am a good person. Anyway, there isn't one there at present.'

'It is shameful to brag of what you cannot fulfil,' Finn said reprovingly to the small men. Then he went white as the pain worsened and his head burned. The next moment the pain was gone and Finn looked out with new eyes and a wide smile at the world and everything in it.

'I had a headache,' he said.

'I have it here in my hands,' the thief said. He opened his cupped hands and a small black thing jumped up, gave a small scream and faded away.

Finn was delighted. He bent down without fear of pain and he hugged the little man, shook him by the hand and asked his name.

'I am Taking Easy,' the small man said.

'No wonder!' Finn said and he hugged him again.

'And who might you be?' he then asked the next small man.

'I am Climber!' the small man said.

'What can you climb?'

'I can climb anything; there's nothing I can't climb. I can go up glass as if I were born a fly. I can skip up the sheerest waterfall, hopping from drop to drip. I can stride up a sunbeam. And Finn Mac Cool, I could even climb up a line drawn in the air by your finger!'

'Do it!' said Finn, making a line in the air.

Climber twinkled up the invisible, insubstantial line and sat on its impossible top, grinning widely. Then he slid back down to stand beside Finn again, if possible with a broader grin than before.

'Could you do it twice?' Finn asked.

'I could,' said Climber; and he did.

'That was well done,' said Finn most heartily; and turning to the seventh small man, he asked:

33

'What about you?'

'If I sit down – no one can get me up,' the small man said.

'Gariv could,' Finn interjected with a wry smile.

'Gariv nor a hundred Garivs couldn't!' the small man laughed. 'As well, if I take hold of something while I'm sitting down, nothing at all can take it away from me and the greatest strength in the whole world couldn't pull away from my clasp.'

'And what's your name?'

'I'm Lazy Back.'

'Sit down, Lazy Back, until we try your word and your strength!'

Lazy Back sat down and he offered Finn his hand. With his two hands, Finn took a grip of Lazy Back's hand and arm and began to pull. As he began to pull, he felt the very tissue in Lazy Back's hand and arm change. It became rocklike and was a deadweight, inert and unhuman. At first Finn barely exerted his own strength, fearing to hurt the small man; but in a short time he dug in his heels and he tugged and laboured until the sweat ran in rivers down his back, and not a stir could he get out of the laughing small man. Lazy Back was heavier than a mountain.

Finn gave up in the end and wiped the sweat from his face.

'You're well named,' he said and he turned a red

34

but smiling face to the last of the small men.

'My name is Three Sticks and I can make anything at all that you'd name, out of wood,' the small man said.

'I believe you,' said Finn. 'But surprise me, anyway.'

Three Sticks threw a small twig high up into the air. When it had spun very high, he said:

'Hawk!'

The stick grew wings, legs and a head. It filled out and covered itself with feathers. It was a hawk and it flew away.

Three Sticks threw a small piece of wood on to the land. It spun through the air and at the moment of landing, Three Sticks said:

'Deer!'

There was a flurry about the stick and four delicate legs touched the ground and a beautiful young female deer ran away.

'Could you make a ship?' Finn asked.

Three Sticks tossed a twig on to the breathing sea and a fine ship was there rising and falling in the water.

'Now,' said Knowing Man. 'We have given

accounts of ourselves and we already know why you are here and where you want to go. We would like to take service with you, Finn; and help the King of the big men.'

'I suppose you knew about it all the time?' Finn asked.

'He did – as I did,' Far Feeler answered, nodding.

'Lucky for me that I met you!' said Finn.

He then carried the small men two by two out to the ship, not surprised at all that Lazy Back was no heavier than the others when he wasn't using his talent. When everyone was on board, they raised the sail, and away they went to sea.

Far Feeler took his position at the prow of the ship and he said:

'I can see where we must go. I can see the small marks in the water where the keel of the giant's ship parted the waves. The track is easy for me to follow.'

Bowman took the rudder and Lazy Back took charge of the sail and under the guidance of Far Feeler, the ship went along at a great lick. By afternoon, they had gone seven leagues and a bit and a fair country appeared before them. Knowing Man said that this was the country of the giants, so the sail was taken down, the ship was beached and the voyagers jumped down on to the shore. They tied up the boat and set out through the countryside to make their way to the castle of the King.

What a country it was!

There were bees as big as cushions and mushrooms like great platters and butterflies like

incredibly coloured flying table-cloths, well starched. In the hedges, the wild plums were bigger than turnips and the honeysuckle hung in large, curly, pink trumpets; and the scent was like the fumes of a strong but sweet wine. Once they saw a wasp and it was so horribly dangerous-looking that they all hid in the bushes until it passed by, even Finn! When they couldn't hear its awesome whine any more, they emerged from their hiding-place and stepped out again for the castle. After a while, the perfume from the honeysuckle was so overpowering that each man pinched his nose tightly for fear of falling into a trance and, before long, they reached the castle's outer defences and wondered how any thief could pass them.

First there was a wide expanse of gravel that a rabbit couldn't skitter over without drawing sharp attention to itself. Next there was an encircling sweep of a wall with spikes. The spikes bristled out with the thickness of the spines on a hedgehog's back, and they bristled up into the air as well from the top of the wall, and they shone from sharpening and caught the light. As far as could be seen, there was only one door in the spiked wall and that door bristled like a hairbrush.

A watch was being kept for Finn; and when he and his friends were seen after they had taken only two scrunchy steps over the gravel, the door opened

and a sentry giant came out to welcome Finn and take him on in through the rest of the defences. He barred the way at first, with his great sword very nervous in his hands, until Finn had given his word that the small men were of good will and that they had come to help protect the new-born child. Finn said nothing of their skills; he thought it best not to mention that Taking Easy was a member of the thief class for fear that the huge man might lose control of his great sword and it would get fidgety again.

The giant led them in through the open door.

On the other side of the spiked wall, there was an unsuspected plunging drop to a broad ditch where sharp stone teeth stood upright. It was like the skeletal bottom jaw of a monstrous fish. Finn and his friends were led over a bridge of thick planks and when they were all safely across, the giant lifted the planks and carried them on his shoulders.

Now there was an area of grass, where, in earlier and happier times, the King and Queen used to sunbathe and make garlands of flowers for each other's heads and play tiddley-winks, the sentry remembered and told sadly to Finn and his small men. But many sentries with fierce hounds on leashes walked there now; and the sentries held their flashing swords in their hands and looked to be ready for anything. Finn thought them all unusually handsome for giants, as the ones he had encountered up until this were ugly enough to frighten wart-hogs and come last, and well last, in any beauty competition. These giants had bronzed, good-looking faces, but they all had very grave expressions and their manner of walking was very solemn, because they knew that they had an important duty to perform for their beloved King and Queen. The honour and responsibility of this task showed in their bearing. Even so, they all relaxed a little bit on seeing Finn and few could suppress smiles at the sight of the small men. Finn was pleased to notice that even their teeth looked quite reasonable.

When this second area was crossed, there was a deep, deep moat that was as wide as a small river. The King's great castle stood on the other side. There was no way to cross until their sentry-friend laid the planks, and when this was done and the planks were tested, they all followed him over the water to the heavy door where more sentries stood. A few words of explanation were exchanged and then the welcome visitors were taken into the presence of the King and announced as:

'Finn Mac Cool and Small Friends!'

The poor King was in a strange muddle of feelings. He was overjoyed because of the birth of his new little son, he was in terror of the secret thief, and he was happy and relieved that Finn had come.

'O Finn! O Small Friends!' he said.

His emotions got the better of him and he could say no more. His body servant ran to cuddle him and lead him to his throne where he helped him to sit down.

'There, there!' he said, just as Gariv would in times of stress.

The King was different from all of the other giants in that he had a long, silky, milk-white beard, and this he began twisting and curling and screwing round his fingers, as he sobbed and said:

'Ah, my babbies! Oh, my dear little dotes! Ah, my lovely boys!'

The tears brimmed out of his eyes, they coursed down his cheeks and in a very little time, they drenched his beard.

'You'll think me unmanly, I know . . .' the King began; but Finn swallowed and said gruffly:

'I'm a father myself, O King.'

The King accepted this as a gracious gift and he struggled with his feelings until he managed to give Finn a smile. It was difficult to interpret it as a smile at all, being very wan indeed and smothered by whiskers, but Finn recognized it for what it was and smiled back encouragingly.

'Ah, then you'll understand,' said the King. 'You'll understand the feelings of a father with two lovely little sons already plucked from under our very noses and no one with the faintest idea of who did the snatching, or why. They were kidnapped, you know,' he finished in a whisper.

'I know,' Finn said, and once more he wondered how in the world any thief could get past the defences and the guards.

'My firstborn was a beautiful boy – took after his mother,' the King said fondly. 'He had glorious eyes that were so soft and beautiful you'd want to drown in them – full of wonderful colour, you know. My second boy was just the same. And now we have this third prince – a little bloomer. Skin like pink peonies, Finn,' the King finished with a loud sob.

He burst into tears again and when he was over the worst and at the sobbing stage he choked out:

'Here today and gone tomorrow!' and he looked beseechingly at Finn.

'There, there,' Finn now found himself saying.

'Have you just the one son?' the King asked.

'I have a grandson, too,' Finn answered, feeling almost guilty.

'How lucky you are!' the great King said.

'I know it,' said Finn.

'You can put your arms around them any time you want to; but tomorrow, I'll be holding out my arms to empty air. The thief will surely come! It will be the end of me and the end of my heart-broken Queen! Lift this curse from us, Finn,' the great King pleaded.

43

Finn's heart expanded with pity for the King and his Queen. Far Feeler could stand it no longer and he was sobbing roughly with his hands over his face.

Finn stood as straight as a spear shaft and laid his hand across his breast.

'I swear by the oath my people swear by that you shall not lose this child,' he said, and that was his most solemn word.

'Oh, thank you,' the King said with a simple frankness of manner and voice. 'The Queen will be relieved, so relieved, when she hears.'

'Where is the Queen now?' Finn asked.

'The little woman is in her room having swooning fits. Her servants keep burning feathers and holding them under her nose to bring her round. But every time she is conscious, she asks: "Has Finn Mac Cool arrived yet?" and "Is it morning now?" and on hearing that you haven't and it isn't, she flops out again, poor darling,' the King answered, and he started to cry afresh.

Suddenly, there was an almighty crashing sound from just above them.

'There she goes once more, poor sweetheart,' said the King to Finn.

'It would be better if she were left in peace,' Finn said.

'She didn't want that,' the King explained ingenuously. 'She wanted to be told the exact moment of your arrival. Oh dear! With all my upset, I've forgotten to send word that you're here. I'm a selfish beast, I am!'

'Tell the servants to leave off burning feathers, tell them to stand by her and wait with her until morning. Let the Queen sleep!' said Finn.

'Finn is here, let the Queen sleep!' the King commanded, and word went swiftly to the Queen's room and the poor lady was given a sleeping potion by a giant of the medical Druid class and was left to her troubled dreams.

'Where is the new-born infant?' Finn asked next.

'With the Queen at present, well guarded in her bed-chamber. Before dusk, he will be taken to the strongest room in the castle. Much good it will do!' the King answered, and he looked at Finn with eyes that brimmed again and added: 'No offence, of course.'

'Take him to the strongest room now and we shall go at once and be his guard,' Finn said, feeling slightly challenged.

'We can't, not yet – the Queen likes to look at him,' the King explained.

'As soon as the Queen is asleep, then it can be done and we'll take up our duty to him and to you,' Finn said.

'Oh dear me, no!' the King exclaimed with regal shock. 'That would never do. First we must have the usual banquet, you know. Only a matter of a few sides of beef, a bit of pork, a drop of soup, a morsel of venison and a toast to the Queen and the babby, do you see? And we must have the normal "welcome strangers" sort of do. We must have it. It's a question of custom and doing the right royal thing. The Queen would be quite put out if we didn't have it, the little woman would be very upset and I'd never hear the end of it, you know.'

'But the thief might come,' Finn suggested.

'The thief never, ever, comes until it is pitch-black night; and if we hurry with the feasting, we should be done well before dusk.'

The King got up from his throne and led Finn and his small companions into the feasting-hall. It was already packed out with seated giants: men, women and children. They were the nobility, and they all stood up and bowed as the King and his guests passed by and walked to the top table. There was a rustle of interest and curiosity from this great assembly that sounded like a forest of dried oatstalks being shaken by a wind. All looked at Finn first and then they stared at the small men, fascinated. All necks craned to see them and the King blushed for shame. The small men smiled and bowed in all directions and they didn't lose one jot of their composure and their dignity.

At the top table, there was another throne for the

King and a seating arrangement had been made for Finn and the small men. Two heavy wooden chairs had been placed facing away from each other and a bench had been created by resting a plank between them through their high ladder-backs. The King's body servant came and lifted a red-faced Finn and his small men up to sit on the plank. All eyes were fastened on the small men.

'Are they gobbelings?' a childish voice asked loudly in the silence.

This was answered by a fierce whisper of:

'Hush! Manners!'

Then the child giant said even more
loudly:

'I want one!'

This time the answer was a threat of bed without supper while the King looked pained.

He coughed once in a noble manner and all of the giants instantly stopped staring and did other things, like examining their cutlery and their finger-nails with deepest interest.

The workboxes of all the ladies in the castle had been raided for thimbles as vessels for the guests, the silver ones being laid in place of goblets and the ones made of china, for soup. As no spoons could be found that were small enough to be of any use, short pieces of hollow straw were provided; and the King whispered that he and protocol would not be offended by noise and that they could suck away to their hearts' content. But Finn pointed out that their mouths could not possibly fit round such great straws, and asked if they could dip bread instead. The King looked relieved and said, still whispering:

'That will be fine.'

Now that everyone and everything was settled, the King called for the feasting to begin.

'Draw in to the table and dive in,' he said to his people in a formal and time-honoured way.

Everyone immediately tried to be cheerful; but the King was so tightened up with anxiety and sadness that a cloud hung over everything and people were jumpy. The short-lived relief of being curious about the small men was gone.

The servants were all bags of nerves.

They came in bearing cauldrons of soup, joints of pork, beef and venison, both roasted and boiled, rafts of bread slices as big as paving-stones, and nicely browned chickens and other fowl, each one big enough to feed six normal men of good appetite. They dropped and spilled a lot of things, and the solemn-faced company was kept busy ducking and dodging boiling soup and hot gravy and sizzling joints of meat, but no one complained. The feast was set in vast quantities on all of the tables and all the food steamed upwards and the steam was like a fog where an ordinary-sized ship might be lost.

'We know how to keep ourselves happy,' the King said, trying to be jolly, and he promptly burst into tears again. Other soft-hearted giants burst into tears as well. Then there was a great sobbing and a powerful blowing of noses like foghorns in many keys and the noise rose to the rafters and echoed back. It was all quite wretched. The giants that hadn't burst into tears just looked deeply depressed.

The King cried like a sluice and his hot salty tears fell into his soup and ruined it completely. It went as thin as rain and all of his bread went to slush. A servant came and removed it all, as it wasn't fit for ultrahuman consumption and would have to be used as animal-food. The servant's nerves were so bad with worry and distress

that he dropped the King's special soup plate and smashed it to bits.

'May all our bad luck go with it!' Finn said loudly and everyone was pleased.

With his own hands, the King cut slices of meat for his honoured guests, and he cut the slices into little pieces, as if for children, and he offered this food on small pieces of bread to the small men and Finn. Finn went as red as a beetroot with embarrassment, for he was the Great Finn, the Chieftain of the Fianna and a giant among his own kind; but he covered up for himself by remarking casually on the weather.

'Isn't it hot today?' he said, as inscrutably as he could.

He took a half-hearted bite of bread and meat and struggled to swallow it. But the whole banquet was infected by the King's melancholy and Finn had a lump in his throat that made eating and swallowing a difficult thing to do. He was surprised to see that his small friends were munching cheerfully and asking for more. Not to show bad manners and disappoint the King and the watching cooks, he persisted with the mouthful and managed to get it down.

A messenger came to say that now the Queen was deeply asleep and the infant prince had been taken to the strongest room in the castle, under a guard of the toughest giants and with his two nurses in attendance.

'It'll do no good,' the King muttered, his head dropping forward in dejection. He expelled a great sigh.

In the end it had to be admitted that the banquet was a washout, for the King's harpers, being artistic and sensitive above the common run of aristocratic giants that were present at the feast, couldn't sing a straight note for sheer misery, and couldn't do a trill, for their sobbing had made their breath control go to pot; and they kept saying: 'We feel it more,' until everyone got tired of their noise and withdrew from the feasting-hall, some still blowing noses and blotting eyes.

◆

Finn and the small men in company with the grieving King were now conducted to the strongest room in the castle, where the new-born child lay fast asleep. Two nurses sat as still as heraldic beasts, one on either side of his cradle; and they were fine-looking women, though of course rather outsize.

Just as soon as the King's party arrived, the guard of toughest giants departed in

some relief, glad to leave the dreadful duty to Finn; not to even mention the respect due to his reputation for high deeds.

Finn at once inspected the room.

It was sparsely furnished without drapes or cupboards where a thief might hide. The only furnishing, apart from the baby's cradle and the chairs where the nurses loomed like statues to dead Queens, was a long table surrounded by chairs, and these were arranged in the centre under a lighted lamp that hung on chains from the ceiling. The table and chairs were of a size rather smaller than might suit Finn; and he guessed that a doll's house somewhere in the castle had been plundered of some of its furniture. In the huge fireplace, a fire of middling-sized tree trunks had been laid but not lit. The walls of the room were easily four feet thick, as could be seen from the embrasure of the one smallish window, where dusk was beginning to show.

Finn went straight to this window and had its shutters closed, barred and bolted before you could say 'snap!' At this, there was the sound of shutters banging all through the castle as the people prepared for the coming of the thief. Keys turned in locks and these keys were then locked in caskets. The caskets were locked in their turn, and their keys were put into leather purses and brought to the King who hung them about his neck. Great fires were lit in the circle between the deep, deep moat and the wall with spikes; and an inner ring of fires surrounded the castle itself. Additional fires blazed on every piece of high ground in the castle's vicinity and all the fires burned brightly through the whole night, replenished scrupulously as bronze gongs sounded the hours, and as needed.

On the walkways of the roof, watchmen were set to watch; and sentries were posted pair by pair below, where they paced and paced in the light of torches that flared from sconces which

were set in the castle's walls. And the pass-word that went from mouth to mouth, was:
'Finn Mac Cool, Mac Baiscne!'

A mouse could not have entered without giving that word.

The King handed a key and a leather bag on a string to Finn, saying:

'Take this. It is the only key that I will not hold tonight. It locks the door of this room, and you, Finn, will lock it after me when I leave and let no one in on any account. You won't, will you?' he finished piteously and with his voice breaking.

'You may trust me,' said Finn. 'My friends and I will guard this child through thick and thin; and if, in spite of all we can do, the child is stolen, then I will certainly answer for it with my head.'

'What more could anyone say!' the King ex-claimed gratefully; and with tears spilling from his eyes, he took a long, devouring, last look at his small son and, crying bitterly, he left the room.

At once Finn locked the door, tested its security by tugging mightily at its latch and, when he was satisfied that it was truly well-locked, he put the key in its bag and hung the bag round his neck. He sat down at the table with the small men and settled himself to wait.

Tension and excitement had filled the castle all day and now Finn was weary of it. He wished for peace and serenity, knowing that these conditions were needed if all his fine instincts and qualities were to work unhindered. But whenever he glanced at the nurses, he was dismayed; for the tension and excitement still lived inside them and their eyes glittered with anxiety and their bodies were stiff with fear.

At last he said in part vexation:

'You can sleep safely, ladies. Leave the guarding and the worry to us, the trusted servants of your King.'

And at once, the nurses exhaled long sighs and they seemed to deflate somewhat; and in no time at all, the release from distress brought sleep, for they were desperately tired.

Soon they were asleep so deeply that their bottom lips rippled from the force of their breathings out; and two breezes came from them that made the hanging lamp swing to and fro and caused shadows to chase each other all around the room.

Then it was that Knowing Man spoke quietly to Finn.

'You shouldn't have offered your head for that little lad's safety, for he will be snatched tonight, in spite of all we can do,' he said.

'You took your time telling me; why didn't you tell me before?' Finn asked with some exasperation.

'If I told everything I know – no one would ever do anything,' Knowing Man said with a smile.

'Don't *smile* at me, *tell* me! Do you know who the thief is?' Finn said sternly.

'She's the King's own sister! She's a spiteful old biddy of a witch and she lives far away in her own castle on the top of a glassy mountain. She and the King had a bitter quarrel many years ago. The King has forgotten but she has not. She is full to the gills with evil malice and she steals the children for hatred of the King and jealousy of his beautiful Queen,' Knowing Man replied.

'How does she do it with no one seeing her?' Finn asked.

'She makes herself invisible and goes up on the roof. She stretches her hand down the chimney, snatches the child out of its cradle and away she goes without a soul being the wiser. That's how she does it. The King never connects any of his troubles with his own sister. She put it about years ago that she was emigrating to Alba to marry a King over there.'

'Never mind the gossip, light that fire,' said Finn.

And the fire was lit although it was high summer and the night was more than warm.

'When that hand comes down the chimney, I'll take hold of it,' said Lazy Back. 'The hand that comes down, stays down, and that's for sure.'

'Never fear,' Finn said confidently. 'Once she feels the fire, she'll pull away again.'

But in spite of Finn's words, Lazy Back sat down on the floor of the hearth.

'If that child is stolen, there'll be a queer dawn chorus round here in the morning, I'm thinking,' said Bowman after a while.

'I don't know if we should stay at all,' said Taking Easy.

'Maybe we should skedaddle out of here while the going is good and not stay for any drama,' Far Feeler suggested, with his head on one side and looking at Finn with a strange expression.

'Eaten bread is soon forgotten,' said Finn, creating an old saying himself. 'We have eaten at his table, we cannot betray the King. Anyway, I gave my word.'

'But that was when you thought that you were dealing with an honest thief,' Taking Easy pointed out.

'A bargain without full knowledge is no bargain,' Hearing Ear declared.

'That King will make bits of us in the morning!' Three Sticks said.

'The King is a nice man,' Finn said reprovingly.

'He's a King!' said Bowman.

'He can be nice when he wants to be and the other thing when he feels like it,' said Hearing Ear.

'I gave my word,' said Finn.

'We are in the soup then,' said Three Sticks. 'That bad-minded oul biddy of a witch will best us and the King will make us pay.'

'You promised your head, Finn,' Taking Easy reminded him.

'Maybe she won't come. She might be satisfied to have stolen two. We don't know for sure that she will come for the third,' Finn said, without much hope.

'She'll come as sure as a dead goat can't skip,' Knowing Man said emphatically, and he looked strangely at Finn.

'You're a great man for the late word,' Finn said. 'We'll stick it out. You can all go if you want to, but I stay. Don't mention skedaddling to me any more!'

His sudden thoughts were of Oisín and Oscar and his heart was with the King.

The small men exchanged smiles with each other.

'We'll stay,' Three Sticks said. A small piece of wood in his hands turned into a gaming board with pieces.

'We can play chess to pass the time,' Knowing Man said.

'I'm not playing with *you*,' Finn said. 'You're the same as a loaded dice.'

They all sat at the table except for Lazy Back who stayed by the fire. Climber sat opposite Finn and they began to play.

The hours passed by while one played another and all listened for the sound of the witch. Once, a nurse moved in her sleep and the sudden crackle of her starched apron made Finn jump. The baby, too, turned in its sleep, for being a giant his bones were already strong and he could do things like that quite easily. From time to time the sentries below could be heard, walking about, meeting each other, exchanging the password and other words. The nurses snored softly and the swinging lamp continued to cast its running shadows.

The hours crept away.

◆

The mountain of black basalt rock arose in a mass from the sea. From its ponderous base it towered like a steep-sided pyramid until it was high up in the air; and from that airy highness it soared further as a castle with turrets and spires. The castle had been magically carved from the mountain's substance; and its glassy, highly-polished surface sometimes reflected the touch of the moon with a brightness that was like the gleam of pearls. Its rooms were lofty, for the wicked giantess lived there, and its windows were a delicate tracery of the same black stone as its floors and walls. Soft white clouds would, now and then, drift wispily through the rooms in the spires and the turrets. The castle was always cold.

In a room in one of the high spires, the evil

witch paced. She had been twitching with merciless joy all day and constantly wrinkling her long thin nose and her long thin face into the most ghastly of smiles. Once long ago, she had been handsome in common with the giants of  her race, but hatred, jealousy and the sinister thoughts of the dark arts that she practised had written themselves on her face and turned her ugly; malice had almost consumed her body away.

'Not yet dark enough; not yet deep enough,' she repeated over and over, as she observed the sky through the open stonework of her windows.

Once she laughed loudly as she thought of her brother the King.

'Watching for something that he can never see,' she said. 'I am like death itself,' she added, and followed that with a loud whinny of wicked delight.

She darted to a window and looked out, not noticing the sudden withdrawal of two pale areas from the darkness of the window in the spire opposite.

'Soon it will be black night and I can take my pleasure,' she crooned. 'I shall destroy his house, root and branch!'

Away from the window in the opposite

spire, two toddler giants huddled together in the darkness, shivering in their nightshirts.

'What wrong with the Queer One?' the younger whispered, using one of the many names they called her when she was not present.

Although he was very, very young, and his brother not much older, they were both able to speak quite well, for their witch aunt had taught them both a lot, in the matter of speech and understanding. Not from the kindness of her heart had she done this thing; but there was no fun in taunting infants, as she had found out when she tried it first on the older of the stolen boys. She had said terrible things to him and all that he had done in reply was smile and chuckle and allow his baby dribbling to make bubbles on his lips that he could pop.

'I seen her like this before,' the older one said. 'Next day, you was here.'

'Stoled, I was,' the younger one said sadly.

'Like me. I was stoled first.' The older one explained patiently the fact of his precedence, as he always did, when this was discussed.

'Stoled by Knag The Hag,' the smaller one said and he giggled.

'Ssshh!' said the older one. 'If she hear us, she might give us clumps on the head.'

'Us ones gets lots of clumps 'cos she doesn't love us,' the smaller one said sadly. 'She doesn't love us 'cos of our father, the King.'

'That's right. 'Member what she said after you was stoled?' the older one asked.

' "I am a saucer," she said, "an' I have stoled you by magic from your father, the King. I hates him and I don't love you, you can be certain of that," she said and she did one of her laughs.'

'She said: "I am a sauceress," not a saucer,' said the older one. 'I'm *glad* she don't love us even if it clumps.'

'She kiss me this morning,' the younger one said with a shudder.

'She bin strange all day,' the older one said, knowingly. 'She near blew the eardrums out of my head when I asks more porridge for me supper.'

'She kiss me this morning,' said the younger one again. 'She said us ones were a blessing to her and she laugh very strange. I hates her.'

'I hates her too and I hates that porridge,' the older one whispered vehemently. 'It's always cold and lumpy. Not like the great feeds they do be having at our father's castle.'

'We only got milk there,' the younger reminded him.

'That's 'cos we had no teeth,' said the older boy.

'If we had teeth what would we get?' the younger one asked and he wriggled in his nightshirt with anticipation.

'They does be having poke, an' beef and chickens. And bread and soup every day. I 'member how I could smell it all when they was celebrating me. She has all them things for her dinner but we never get none,' the older one complained.

'Say what you 'member about Daddy the King,' the younger one begged and he wriggled again.

'Well,' the older one began slowly as if trying to remember, although this was their favourite conversation and they had it at least once a day, usually saving it up for when they were in bed at night and safe from the witch's hearing.

'Yes?' the younger one questioned eagerly.

'Well,' the older one said slowly again, drawing it out. 'He was a big fellow with whiskers.'

'Them whiskers was wet,' the younger said quickly.

'They was not. They was long and soft and ever so warm,' the older boy said firmly.

'They was wet the night I was borned,' the younger one insisted.

Now the older one wriggled with joy.

'Why was that?'

'He was crying,' the younger one said. 'He was crying 'cos you was stoled away. I heard him say it.'

'He's a kind Daddy,' the first-born said. His lip trembled and his voice wavered. 'I wish I was with him in his castle.'

'It's clumps if you cry, don't cry,' the younger one said. 'Me too. I wish us ones was with the kind Daddy – 'specially 'cos we got teeth now.'

From the spire across from them, there was a shrilling of laughter. The stolen boys ran and scrambled into bed, pulling the thin covers over their heads.

The witch had laughed because the night sky had gone thick with heavy cloud. She stood in the middle of the black stone floor and prepared to leave. Her preparation began by the taking of a stance.

Her eyes were bright with madness.

◆

Far Feeler suddenly sat bolt upright and said:
'The witch is getting ready.'

'What is she doing?' whispered Finn.

'She stands strangely in the centre of a room. Her arms are outstretched and she mutters a spell. She has one eye going east and one eye going west, not looking outwards but inwards, as if they would cross over the bridge of her nose and swap places. She has one foot pointing north and one foot pointing south and she is beginning to twist. Now she is twisting and spiralling up into the air and now she has vanished.'

'She is in the sky and on her way,' said Knowing Man.

'How's that fire?' asked Finn.

'Blazing,' said Lazy Back.

'Throw on a few more of those young trees to make it really high,' Finn ordered.

'Don't bother,' said Three Sticks and he took a chip of wood from his pocket and tossed it on to the wood that already blazed and in the same second the fire was flashing and roaring up the chimney.

Then Far Feeler said:

'She is coming over the sea.'

A short while later he exclaimed with growing excitement:

'She is fast approaching; she moves like a dart.'

'Steady yourself,' said Finn. 'Everyone keep a cool head and keep a good watch on that chimney.'

He and the other small men went and stood in a curve by the roaring fire, forming a guard line from where Lazy Back was sitting.

'She's arrived,' Knowing Man said. 'She's over the gravel; she's over the spikes; she's over the sentries on the grass; she's over the moat; she has landed on the ground for the pleasure of walking with the guard just below us; she's invisible.'

'Her pleasure will be short-lived; she doesn't know we're here,' Finn said grimly.

'I can feel the shaking of her silent laugh- ter,' Far Feeler said wincing. 'It is very evil. Step by step and in mimicry, she walks with a pair of unsuspecting guards. Now she is spiralling up in the air.'

'Still invisible, she floats above, looking down at the useless defences,' Knowing Man said. 'Laughing aloud now, but very softly, she views the sentries with contempt.'

'Now she is on the roof,' Far Feeler whispered; and a feeling of great danger invaded Finn. This was not like a fair fight where an enemy was faced man to man.

'Get ready!' he said. He didn't know what for; but he said it anyway.

The very next instant the arm of the giantess was down the chimney, with its hand spread ready to grope for the child. It was still invisible but the flames licked it, there was the smell of frazzled hair to betray it, and then it was withdrawn, without the King's small son and without a sound being made.

'She's been stung a little bit,' Finn said with some relief. He wondered what would happen next.

The witch pulled a small piece of cloud across the sky and when it was over the chimney she squeezed it like a full sponge and rain came flooding down to put out the fire. The room filled with steam.

With great bravery all of the small men held their arms in the chimney opening and when the arm came down again, it did not escape detection. Lazy Back caught hold of it quite gently and he exerted his full strength. He was far, far heavier and stronger

68

than the basalt mountain where the witch's castle stood.

The witch never made a single sound all through this contest of strength. She pulled, and Lazy Back held on. The muscles on the arm stood out in long hard lumps and the veins bulged and were as thick vines going up a tree trunk, but these things could not be seen by Finn and the small men. The witch knew them and felt them, and she tried with all of her might to pull away from whatever strange thing it was that had caught such a hold of her. After a while, drips of sweat ran down the arm and dropped to the hearth making dark spots as big as saucers in the ashes. Still there was no sound in the room but for the nurses' gentle snoring and the child's breathings in and out. The lamp swung but it could hardly be seen through the steam. All eyes were on Lazy Back's fearsome handclasp.

Suddenly Lazy Back tipped over. The witch's pull had gone and, at a stroke, the arm was visible. It had come away from its socket in the witch's shoulder and now it was lumpishly blocking the chimney.

Everyone was stunned at this awful thing, but at the same time glad; for now Finn would not lose his head; they had won the battle and the infant was still safe. The arm was dragged down into the room by the small men and everyone stood marvelling at it, and they congratulated themselves in whispers on having beaten the witch, for surely she had gone after such wounding, and the danger was past.

And while they stared at the arm and talked, the second arm came swiftly and invisibly through what remained of the steam, snatching the infant prince before anyone could say 'snip!'

All were aghast. Disaster had come so swiftly that even Knowing Man was stunned. Everybody had seen the well-wrapped infant prince fly across the room through the dispersing steam and shoot up the chimney. They looked at the empty cradle and at the empty fireplace; they stared at each other with total disbelief.

Finn was the first to recover.

'Quick!' he hissed. 'We'll follow her to her castle over the sea!'

He took the key from its bag and opened the door. They all left on tiptoe, with Finn locking the door after them as quietly as he could.

Now the castle's defences had to be breached but luckily the giants were watching for a thief to break in and were not expecting anyone to try to break out, so their greatest attention was given outwards. As soon as Finn and his men reached the door of the castle and had opened it stealthily – no difficulty there, Taking Easy simply stole the locks – Bowman got to work. He released an arrow that went silently and swiftly all around the right-hand side of the castle. It extinguished all the lights and fires.

Immediately, the giants on the left-hand side snatched the torches from their sconces and ran in a thunderous rush of mighty bodies and great feet, to where they believed the thief was trying to steal in under cover of darkness. Bowman's second arrow put out all the fires on the left-hand side, the torches were already gone and now black night was all around the castle. His third arrow struck out the fires burning on the surrounding hills and in an instant there was no light at all. Giants ran everywhere in solid, thudding clusters, treading on dogs that yelped, and colliding in groups from moment to moment. During all this commotion and disorder, Three Sticks threw a twig over the moat. A bridge was there to be crossed in a flash, with everyone holding hands so as not to lose each other in the darkness.

Once they were over, Three Sticks bent low and took a twig from the bridge. The bridge promptly disappeared and all ran on to the ditch with the stone teeth and the spiky wall. There, Three Sticks threw his bit of wood. It sailed high up over the wall and there was a second wonderful bridge that spanned not only the wall but the wide expanse of gravel. Just as soon as they had crossed over all the defences, Three Sticks picked up his piece of wood again and the second bridge was no longer there. They were outside without anyone seeing them or being a whit the wiser.

They ran for the beach, holding their noses through the even more stunning night-scent of the honeysuckle, and they had the boat launched and the sail up in double quick time. The sail filled out and the ship moved through the water.

The sea was as black as the sky; not even one star could be seen through the thick substance of cloud. But Far Feeler knew that he could find the way and, with Bowman and Lazy Back at the rudder and the sail as before, the ship glided through the night.

Finn stood with Far Feeler in the prow and he tried to peer ahead, but the darkness seemed to fill his eyes; and if it had not been for the freshness of the air against the skin of his face, his arms and his bare legs, the swishing noise of the sea where the ship cut through the waters and the sporadic flap of the sail in the breeze, he would have thought himself buried deep within the bowels of the earth, far, far from light.

They sailed many miles in the inky silence. Finn's mind ran on Oisín and Oscar and how he would feel if they had been stolen away as infants. He thought of Gariv as well and the many sarcastic remarks he would have to hear from that mouth if he failed in this high deed. At length, one of the small men – he couldn't tell which in the darkness – murmured something about looking up; and when he did, he saw a small tear in the cloud. It all pulled apart and revealed a night sky that glittered with stars and was glorious with a full moon.

They saw the basalt mountain and the witch's castle then, for the moonlight made it a thing of

gleaming spires and turrets that were shining silver
needles in the sky. They took the ship to the far side
away from the light before they made an attempt at
anything else. Very soon it was rising and falling
gently on the dark waters in the shadow of the
mountain with its sail taken down.

'The children are in a room in that spire up
there,' said Knowing Man, pointing. 'They are all
deeply asleep.'

And Climber said to Taking Easy:

'Hop on my back!'

When Taking Easy was settled, Climber went up the side of the mountain as easily as a fly goes up a windowpane but much more directly and very fast. Even though the moonlight did not strike the mountain on this side, there was light enough to see this and to see Taking Easy slip into the room through the tracery of a window.

Taking Easy stole the dreaming younger boy from the tight hold of his sleeping older brother. With Climber's help he brought the boy, still fast away in his dreams, down to the ship and the willing embrace of Finn. While this was happening, the older brother continued to make a loving, protecting circle of his arms, cherishing empty air. A second climb and theft was made and the older boy was with Finn without as much as a flicker of his eyelids or the breaking, for even a second, of the enfolding of his arms around his missing brother. A third climb, and the well-wrapped sleeping infant was rescued

with never a squall. Finn and the small men were delighted that the thefts had gone so well.

They pushed away from the mountain and lifted the sail.

Finn wrapped his cloak around the older boys and set them as comfortably as he could on a spare piece of sail in a niche in the ship's hull. He took the baby  in his arms and held him for as long as he could stand its weight. When Finn got tired, Lazy Back took over and he cuddled the day-old baby that was almost as big as himself. He never felt weary at all.

After a time the movements of the ship awakened the two older boys and they sat wide-eyed and bewildered, feeling very, very shy. They were not used to seeing people of any size whatever, except for their wicked aunt. To them, the small-ness of the small men was a matter of infinite wonder. In their eyes, even Finn seemed to lack natural height.

Finn, glancing and seeing that they were awake,

spoke gently to them, not expecting them to understand a word of what he said, but hoping that they would recognize the tones of his voice as being soothing and friendly.

'It's all right, don't worry,' he said. 'We are taking you to the Daddy and the Mammy and away from that wicked thief for ever.'

The boys said nothing but when Finn wasn't looking, they glanced at each other and smiled.

The night was far gone and the journey nearing its end, when Knowing Man turned to the others and said:

'The witch knows that the children are gone!'

'The anger in her heart is frightful; her whole being is one swirl of rage,' Far Feeler said, broadening their knowledge.

'She is screaming that when she catches up with the thief or thieves, she will bring death with her,' said Knowing Man.

Finn thought of the size of the arm that lay on the floor of the strongest room in the King's castle.

'I wish you hadn't mentioned that,' he said, his voice rather glum.

A strong wind came up.

'Good,' said Finn. 'Give the ship its head and we'll run before it.'

The wind sent the ship faster than a dart; but the witch in the sky was no sluggard either and, by the power of her magic, she was a feverish, impatient streak of speed that could outdo the speed of the wind.

'She is gaining on us,' said Far Feeler. 'She is in her invisible form.'

'Bad news – she'll get us before we know it,' Finn said dolefully. 'There can't be two opinions about that!'

'Not bad news at all,' said Bowman. He fitted an arrow to his bow, getting ready.

'She's drawing level,' said Far Feeler.

Bowman raised the weapon, pulling its string taut.

'She's right above us now, grinding her teeth,' Knowing Man warned.

Bowman waited.

'She's bending her head, ready to begin her swoop!'

Bowman had waited for this.

'Find her evil heart,' he said, releasing the arrow.

78

There was a scream from the witch as the arrow went into her. She died at once and her great thin body was visible, tumbling and twisting and falling with an almighty splash into the ocean, displacing water that went up in great spurts to fall back into a calm sea, the wind having dropped. For a small space of time bubbles came to the surface from the air that was trapped in the witch's clothing. That was the last of her, there was no more witch.

In the light of a gentle dawn the ship was turned for the land of the big men, and

the small men were laughing and doing tricks to please the two boys while the baby still slept.

Finn's relief was beyond telling.

He laughed with the children to see Climber shin up the sail to balance one-footedly on the mast, and to see Three Sticks throw wood chips to the sky where they turned to butterflies and birds; and his laughter was excessively loud. Three Sticks made three toy ships, perfectly matching the one they were in, that was now taking the boys back to hearth and home at last.

'Keep one of these toys for your baby brother to play with when he's older,' Three Sticks said, handing them over. The two boys stared at him, their eyes wide and uncomprehending. The reasoning behind the small man's gifts completely escaped

them, as they had never known a thing called a toy and they had never heard of an action named play.

When they came to land, the boys revelled in their freedom. It was something they recognized instantly. They trotted on ahead, loving the use of their own fat legs, and they looked and picked and sniffed at everything they found. The beautiful castle had been the worst of prisons with never a blade of grass or a flower of any kind to be seen; and now they were free of its cold, confining walls forever.

They looked back frequently for approval as to direction and encouragement in their joyful, un-familiar actions, and these needs were always supplied by Finn and the small men with nods and smiles.

The baby was heavy, so Finn and his friends took turns at his carrying. Finn kept a sharp eye out for wasps and, whenever there was one, they all hid and the boys thought this wonder-fully funny. They laughed as well when the small men and Finn pinched their noses all through the fumes of the honeysuckle, not understanding at all why they did this, as the scent was barely noticeable to themselves.

In full, bright daylight, the castle's outer defences were reached at last. The gravel was all scattered and scuffed from the blundering over it and the falling down on it of the panic-stricken sentry-giants the night before, when they had naturally mistaken the flight of Finn's party for the breaking in of the cruel thief.

The spiked door was thrown wide open.

The lamentation that wafted out was fearsome – a great tumult of noisy weeping, shrieks, sighs and moans – and the air about the castle simply throbbed with the deep sobbing of the giants.

'I said there'd be a queer dawn chorus,' Bowman remarked, under his breath.

As they began to walk across the gravel, their sentry-giant friend looked out dispiritedly, for it mattered not who walked over the gravel now. His face was swollen and his eyes were badly inflamed from crying; and for some long minutes he just stared blankly at Finn, the small men, the boys and the infant. It was as if he couldn't recognize them for what they were; as if he couldn't tell them from rabbits, or pigeons looking for scraps. And then a

light dawned in his eyes and he shouted:

'Tell the King! Tell the King! Finn is here with all the princes and the little men!'

But how could anybody behind the walls do anything other than rush to see for themselves? There was a mad dash to the open door, where in the heat of the moment, two giants were jammed together for some frenzied seconds. When they untangled themselves, they were the first after the giant that

had called out, in the lead of a deliriously joyful stampede that ended with Finn, the small men and the boys being carried shoulder high; and the baby being carried and cuddled by the toughest giant there. No one challenged him for the privilege.

The whole eager procession went triumphantly into the presence of the King.

When he saw what stood before him, the King was speechless. He changed colour several times and then he fainted.

His body servant brought him round by burning feathers under his nose; and when he was conscious, he gazed at his children with loving wonder. Delight began in his eyes, grew a little at his lips as they parted in a smile – one could tell this by watching the outspreading of his whiskers – then it travelled all over his features and his face was radiant. The glitter of fresh tears made his eyes flash like fairy lights; but these were tears of joy.

He held out his arms, the boys were put down and they ran to him. Waves of love overwhelmed the King and his tears fell, swamping his beard entirely. He hugged and kissed his sons until

Finn thought he might kiss their noses flat.

'I haven't enough arms to hug you as I long to do,' he said passionately. 'I wish I was an octopus!'

The boys looked at their father with wide interest. They suddenly grew bold and full of life, since being in their father's arms made them feel at ease and at home.

They touched his face.

'You're a big fellow with whiskers!' the older boy said, quite enchanted.

'Them whiskers is wet!' the younger boy said proudly. His pleasure in having been right was extreme and he looked at his father with fantastic delight.

'Us ones got teeth now,' he said. 'You got any poke?'

'Poke?' the King repeated, amazed, bewildered, delighted and proud.

He looked at Finn and the small men.

'Who stole them from me?' he asked fiercely.

He was horrified to learn that the thief had been his own sister, although he ought to have known, as he admitted ruefully after thinking about it for a while.

'Some King in Alba had a lucky escape!' he remarked waggishly, for now he was like the old self that he thought he never would be again.

He looked at Finn and the small men and his eyes were filled with brotherly love.

'O Finn, O Small Friends,' he said. 'How can I ever thank you? Who can take an act of friendship and weigh it in his hands?'

'No need for thanks, Great King,' said Finn. 'It was all in a day's work.' The King brushed this aside.

'There must be a banquet, at least,' he said, emphatically.

'Oh no!' Finn was polite but hasty with his words. 'Don't trouble yourself.'

'No trouble at all,' said the King. 'It's the least I can do.'

'Oh no,' Finn said again. 'I must be getting back to my own men, before they send search parties to look for me. And Gariv will be worried.' He tried to sound as if he were not pleading.

'The more the merrier! Let your men come and Gariv too; plenty for all,' the King airily insisted.

'But we're not hungry,' the small men said with one voice.

'Not hungry?' the King giant echoed, flabber-gasted.

'Not a bit,' said Finn. 'We thank you and your Queen.'

'The Queen!' the King said, startled. 'Is she awake?'

'She doesn't dare awake for fear of bad news,' said the King's body servant. 'One of the nurses told me that the Queen was moaning and twisting in her sleep with tears constantly soaking into her pillow. And you sit there talking about banquets and a foolish old King in Alba that wanted to marry your cracked sister. Nice goings on, I must say!'

'Hush,' the King said with an embarrassed glance at Finn and an apologetic half-smile.

'You're an old gab!' the servant declared.

'I'm not!' the King answered hotly.

'You are, you always were, and you always will be a gab,' the servant insisted. 'You were a gabby child!'

'Not that again,' said the King.

'You were gabby from your cradle,' the servant declared with an air of remarkable veracity.

Finn was laughing.

'Get to the treasure room at once! See to it that Finn's ship is loaded well and no stinting!' the King ordered. 'You obey my order while I take my small lads to their lovely mother. When she wakes up, they will be the first sight that meets her beautiful eyes.'

'Time you thought of it,' the servant said, getting in the last word before going out.

'That fellow has been mannerly since the first boy was stolen. Now he's at his old tricks again. Being an old servant, he supposes that he can say what he likes,' the King explained, rather sheepishly.

'Is it his natural way?' asked Finn.

'It is,' the King admitted ruefully.

'Then it shows that he is happy. It must mean that things are back to normal,' suggested Finn.

The King's face broke into a wide, enlightened smile.

'It must,' he said.

The King, holding his two older sons, got to his feet. Farewells were made then and everyone said that they thought the world of everyone else. Shouting out lovely things about friendship, the King left for the Queen's room, followed by the toughest giant who still carried the baby.

Finn and the small men were taken shoulder high to the strand, where they found the ship dipping under the weight of treasure the King had ordered; and the King's servant was there with a silver spoon that he was sending as a gift to Gariv.

Giants towed the ship out to sea and gave it a gentle push, and in no time at all the land of the big

men had disappeared on the horizon and the boat was scraping the sand of the familiar beach where Finn had first met his small friends.

He jumped ashore and turned to lift them to land, but they were gone, with not a sign or sight of them anywhere. If not for the ship still lying low in the water, he might have believed that they had never been there at all and that everything had been a dream.

Leaving the ship to be unloaded later, he set off for the camp of the Fianna, carrying Gariv's present.

The men were all sitting about waiting for him, playing Cat's Cradle and doing all the kill-time things they had done before, with many bored sighs. They received Finn and his story with eagerness, excitement, and envy at not being there with him, and they were overwhelmed and bursting with pride to hear of the high deed that had been done. Gariv listened proudly with the others, taking it all in better than most, perhaps – while at the same time he admired his fine silver spoon.

In the silence that fell after the story was told, he couldn't stop himself saying:

'The small men did a lot – what did you do?'

Finn smiled.

'I gave the orders,' he said and waited.

'That's you all over,' said Gariv and he did not understand at all why Finn laughed and clasped him in a hug and danced him round the fire.

Nor did any of the Fianna.

THE BEWITCHING OF ALISON ALLBRIGHT

Alan Davidson

Alison has always sought refuge in day-dreams: of a lovely home, of being an exciting person, of doing all that the others at school do – and more. Dreams ... until Mrs Considine appears, spinning her amazing web of fantasy, creating another life for Alison out of those dreams. There is no magic in the bewitching of Alison Allbright, only the hypnotically dazzling lure of that other life. Until it's clear enough to see clearly.

STAN

Ann Pilling

Stan couldn't have been more unlucky in running away from his London foster home, for he gets unwittingly caught up in the activities of vicious criminals and is pursued by one of them who will stop at nothing to get what he wants. But throughout his terrifying journey to Warrington and Liverpool and across the Irish Sea, Stan never loses hope of the determination to find his brother and the home he dreams of.

DREAM HOUSE

Jan Mark

For Hannah, West Stenning Manor is a place of day-dreams, but for Dina its attraction lies in the celebrities who tutor the courses there. But when a well-known actor arrives, hotly pursued by his attention-seeking daughter Julia, Dina begins to realize that famous people are no better than ordinary ones. A warm and tremendously funny story by the author of *Thunder and Lightnings*.